SEARCH
AND
RESCUE

SEARCH AND RESCUE

Gail Anderson-Dargatz

RAVEN BOOKS
an imprint of
ORCA BOOK PUBLISHERS

Library and Archives Canada Cataloguing in Publication

Anderson-Dargatz, Gail, 1963–, author
Search and rescue / Gail Anderson-Dargatz.
(Rapid Reads)

Issued in print and electronic formats.
ISBN 978-1-4598-0576-7 (pbk.).--ISBN 978-1-4598-0577-4 (pdf).--
ISBN 978-1-4598-0578-1 (epub)

I. Title. II. Series: Rapid reads
PS8551.N3574S43 2014   C813'.54   C2014-901571-2
C2014-01572-0

First published in the United States, 2014
Library of Congress Control Number: 2014935366

Summary: In this work of crime fiction, Claire Abbott, a small-town
reporter, uses her sixth sense to find a missing girl. (RL 3.0)

*Orca Book Publishers is dedicated to preserving the environment and has
printed this book on Forest Stewardship Council® certified paper.*

Orca Book Publishers gratefully acknowledges the support for
its publishing programs provided by the following agencies:
the Government of Canada through the Canada Book Fund and the
Canada Council for the Arts, and the Province of British Columbia
through the BC Arts Council and the Book Publishing Tax Credit.

Cover design by Jenn Playford
Cover photography by Corbis

ORCA BOOK PUBLISHERS   ORCA BOOK PUBLISHERS
PO Box 5626, Stn. B   PO Box 468
Victoria, BC Canada   Custer, WA USA
V8R 6S4   98240-0468

www.orcabook.com
Printed and bound in Canada.

17 16 15 14 • 4 3 2 1

For Mitch, who remembers me when...

ONE

I felt that familiar ache in my stomach as I drove to my date. I knew something was wrong. More than that, I *knew* I had to head down Pine Road.

The restaurant where my date Trevor waited for me was in the other direction, on Lakeshore. Still, I followed my instincts and turned right. Like it or not, my mother had taught me to take that gut feeling seriously. I was glad I did. When I drove into that quiet suburb, I saw a car burning. The hood was up, and flames burst from the engine.

A young guy stood several yards away, staring at the fire, scratching his head. His eyes were red, like he was about to cry. That beater on fire was likely his first car.

I pulled over and opened my car door. "You okay?" I called across the road.

"I guess," he said. "My car is trashed though."

I got out of my Honda Civic, embarrassed that I showed too much leg. I was dressed for my date, not work. My red skirt was short, cut well above my knees. My high heels made my legs seem even longer.

The kid paused to take me in as I stood. Then he recognized me. "Hey, you're that reporter. You took pictures of my soccer team at the high school this fall."

"That's me," I said. I hunt down stories for our weekly newspaper, the *Black Lake Times*. Today was supposed to be my day off, but here was news.

"Shit," the guy said. "Just my luck. Bad enough this happens. Now everybody will know about it."

He was right. A photo of this car on fire would make the front page.

I grabbed my camera and notepad. Then I slipped on my coat as I walked toward the burning car. We were well into November, and the evening air was cold.

The kid didn't wear a jacket, just jeans and a T-shirt. He shivered. I held out my hand to shake his. "I'm Claire Abbott."

"I know," he said. He wouldn't take my hand. "I see your name in the paper all the time."

I clicked my pen and got ready to jot down his name. "And you are?"

"You can get my name from the cops."

I shrugged off his rude behavior. People often snubbed me. A person in an accident didn't want his photo in the paper. I understood, but this was my job. I had to fill the newspaper every week. In a town as small as Black Lake, that was tough.

I aimed my camera and took a shot of the guy's burning car. "Have you phoned for a fire truck?" I asked him.

"Of course I have," he said. "You think I'm stupid?" He held up his cell phone. "They're on the way."

"If you need anything—"

The teen turned his back on me, not letting me finish.

I waited for the fire truck by my car. I knew I'd get a better photo when the firefighters arrived. I didn't have to wait long. Within minutes, the fire truck wailed down the street and stopped behind the burning car.

The fire chief, Jim Wallis, jumped out. His team of volunteer firefighters followed, all of them wearing their gear. They hooked the truck hoses to the nearest hydrant. With that water, they quickly put out the fire. I got my front-page shot of the firefighters hosing down the flames.

Once the men had the fire under control, the chief crossed the road to see me.

"So Radar strikes again, eh?" Jim asked. "You always have to be the first at a fire, don't you, Claire? You're making the fire department look bad, you know."

Jim called me Radar after that character on the old TV show *M*A*S*H*. Radar was the kid with the teddy bear. He knew what was happening before anyone else did. Like Radar, I was often the first on the scene when someone was in trouble.

Jim shook his head and chuckled. "You're just like your mother."

I cringed. My mother was convinced she was a "remote viewer." She thought she could see with her mind events that were happening far away. Mom often called up the police with "tips" to help them solve their cases.

I knew the cops thought she was a crackpot. Jim was about the only emergency worker in town who took her seriously. Then again, I think he was still a little in love with her. He'd dated Mom after she divorced Dad.

"Believe me," I told him. "I'm nothing like my mother."

Jim gave me a look like he knew better. We both turned back to the young man's blackened car. Smoke and steam still billowed from the engine.

"You hear about the Miller girl?" Jim asked me.

"Helen Miller? The woman who owns the bakery on Lakeshore Road?"

"No, her daughter, Amber." Jim took off his helmet and ran a hand through his hair. "She's missing. She went for a jog on the wilderness trail and got lost. She never came home."

I felt a chill run through me. I *knew* something about that story wasn't quite right.

"She's seventeen," I said, trying to shake off the feeling. "Girls that age forget to phone home. She's likely just hanging out with her boyfriend."

"You mean Doug Conner?" Jim shook his head. "My granddaughter told me they aren't dating anymore. Amber broke up with him a couple of weeks ago. She had a basketball game scheduled for this afternoon. Her mom and her teammates said she'd never miss it."

I hugged myself. "She shouldn't be out in this weather. We're getting snow this evening."

"Exactly," said Jim. "Amber won't last the night in that forest. Search and Rescue is trying to find her now. They've got a camp set up at the foot of Little Mountain."

I felt that familiar tug in my stomach again. "I've got to get over there," I said. I turned away from Jim and opened my car door.

"Hey, what about Trevor?" Jim asked. "He took the day off for your date. I had to scramble to get a replacement."

Trevor was a firefighter, a member of Jim's team. We'd met at a house fire a couple of months earlier. I was first to arrive that time too.

"I'll phone him," I said. When Jim gave me *that* look, I said, "I will. I promise."

Jim knew I'd forgotten to call Trevor when I missed our last date. That time, my gut feeling led me to a car that had just smashed into a power pole. I waited with the driver until the ambulance arrived, then went to the hospital with her. I couldn't leave her alone in that emergency room. She didn't have family.

"There's no point in going to the search-and-rescue camp now," Jim told me. "You'll be one of the first to hear what's happened."

Jim was right. Matt Holden was the search manager for the area. He would send me a press release in the morning. I would use that to write up the story for the paper. Even so, I knew I *had* to get to that search-and-rescue base. I got in my car.

"Matt won't want you there," Jim called through my closed window. "He hates reporters snooping around when they're searching."

I knew that too, but the feeling I had now was stronger than I'd ever had before. I rolled down my window. "I've got to get over there," I told Jim. "If I don't, that girl won't leave that forest alive."

TWO

As I drove to the camp I grew even more certain I had to help find Amber. If I didn't, I knew she would die. I had no idea how I knew. I just did. I had never been surer of anything in my life.

The search-and-rescue base camp was set up at the foot of Little Mountain. The mobile command unit was an old school bus painted white. From that bus, Matt Holden planned the search and told volunteers what to do.

I knocked lightly on the bus door, and Matt opened it. He seemed even taller than usual, staring down at me from the top of those stairs. He wore work boots and his orange search-and-rescue gear. I felt ridiculous coming to this camp in my miniskirt and heels.

"What the hell are you doing here?" Matt demanded.

Hello to you too, I thought as I climbed into the bus. When we'd first met, I had hoped Matt would ask me out. I liked his honest, frank manner, not to mention his rugged good looks. He was fair-haired and muscular. My mother called him "the Viking."

However, I'd quickly realized he didn't much like me. More to the point, he didn't like reporters.

"I saw the chief at a car fire just now," I said. "He told me Amber Miller is missing."

"Ambulance chasing again, were you?" Matt asked.

"Actually, I was on my way to dinner," I said. "I just happened on the accident."

That wasn't quite true, of course. I had followed my intuition—my gut feeling—to that burning car. Matt didn't need to know that. He would think I was as crazy as my mom.

"Out on a date, huh?" he said. He glanced down at my miniskirt. "That explains the getup." He turned away as he continued talking, as if he was uncomfortable. "You're seeing that firefighter now, right? Trevor Bragg."

His question surprised me. Matt rarely asked about my personal life. Then again, before Trevor I didn't have much of a life outside work. I hadn't dated anyone in over a year.

I pulled my notepad from my camera bag. "I take it you haven't found Amber yet?" I asked. "What time did she go missing?"

I was a reporter, just doing my job. I was also trying to figure out why I was here.

I knew I had to help save Amber. But how was I supposed to do that?

Matt sighed, impatient with me. "I'll email you a press release in the morning."

"I'm here now," I said. "Can't you take a few minutes to fill me in?"

Matt scratched behind his ear. "Fine. Amber went jogging on these trails after lunch. She didn't return. That's her car over there. She was only wearing a light jacket, and we found that along the trail. Before she left, she told her mother she wouldn't be out long."

"Is her mother here?" I asked. "Can I talk to her?"

"I sent Helen home to get some rest." Matt glanced at me sideways, like he knew what I was thinking. "Don't call her on your cell. She's scared out of her wits. The last thing she needs is some newspaper reporter asking a bunch of questions."

"No, of course not," I said. Although that was what I'd planned to do. "Do you think Amber is simply lost? Or was she kidnapped?"

"Kidnapped?"

I wrote on my notepad as I talked. "Is there any reason to believe someone took her?"

Matt eyed me. "Do you have any reason to believe that?"

"Well, no." I stopped writing, wondering why I had asked. The question had just popped out of my mouth.

Matt leaned over a map of the wilderness trails. "Look, can we do this in the morning? As you can imagine, I'm a little busy at the moment."

"May I at least take a picture of the jacket Amber was wearing? If she isn't found tonight, we could run the photo in the paper. Maybe someone saw her in it."

Matt thought a moment. "That may be useful," he said. He pulled the jacket from a box and laid it on the table. "But I will find her tonight." He sounded determined, but I also heard the worry in his voice. Amber had been missing for several hours, and the sun had just set.

"You can run her photo too," he said. He handed me her high-school picture. Amber was a pretty girl, with long blond hair. Her skin was fair and her eyes were blue. She was taller than most girls her age. Her height made her a natural for basketball.

I tucked the photo into my camera bag. Then I turned to Amber's jacket. The high-school basketball team crest was on the back. "Her team jacket," I said, reaching for it.

"She plays center," he said.

As soon as I held the jacket in my hands, I got the oddest sensation. I felt like I was going down a waterslide, inside one of those tubes. I was excited, but scared too. The feeling only lasted a moment.

Then, weirdly, I saw Amber. Her image was in the bus window in front of me, like she was on TV. I had a vision of her.

She was lying on the ground. Her hair was over her face. I saw bruises on her arm. She was several feet from the edge of a cliff.

As suddenly as the vision started, it was gone. Instead of Amber's image, I saw my own face reflected in the bus window. My curly brown hair, my heart-shaped face, my brown eyes.

Mom had told me about her visions. What had just happened to me was like what she described. I never really believed her though. I thought she imagined things, or worse. I thought she might be losing her mind.

But I knew my vision was real. Amber was out there, lying injured on the cold ground. I had to find her.

For the first time in my adult life, I believed my mother was a remote viewer.

She could reach out to distance places with her mind. Evidently, I could too.

The thought terrified me. I felt so woozy that I dropped Amber's jacket and almost fell down myself.

"Whoa," said Matt. He grabbed me. "Are you all right? Here, sit down." He offered me a folding lawn chair.

"I'm fine," I said. I sat down anyway. "I haven't eaten since breakfast. I guess I'm hungrier than I thought." I didn't want to tell him what had really happened. He would think I was seeing things and going crazy.

"You better go meet Trevor for that dinner date then," he said.

"Trevor!" I cried. "He's been waiting in that restaurant all this time. Shit. I forgot all about him."

Matt grinned and shook his head. "I won't tell him you said that."

"No, please don't."

"You better phone him," said Matt. "I'll grab a coffee and leave you to it." He turned to get off the bus.

"Matt, wait," I said. I paused. I knew I was about to embarrass myself in front of Matt and likely the whole town. Word got around quickly in this small community. Everyone would think I was as nutty as my mom.

I was also convinced that if I said nothing about my vision, Amber would be dead by morning.

I stood to face Matt, my hands shaking. He crossed his arms as he waited for me to say something. How could I explain? I didn't really understand what was happening myself. Even so, I knew I had to try.

I took a deep breath and spit it out. "I think I know where Amber is," I said.

THREE

"If you knew where Amber is, why didn't you tell me?" Matt's face reddened with anger. He was intimidating when he was pissed. He tried to stand to his full height and bumped his head on the bus ceiling.

"I didn't know until just now," I said. "I mean, I had this feeling—"

Matt glared down at me. He was head-and-shoulders taller than me. "You had a *feeling*?" He paused. "You mean like one of your mother's crazy hunches?"

Here we go, I thought. This was exactly the reaction I had feared. I realized then that

I had to be sure of Amber's location before I tried to explain further. I also needed some proof to convince Matt that what I'd seen was real. Otherwise, he wouldn't believe me.

"Can I just hold Amber's jacket again?" I asked.

"Why?"

"Humor me," I said.

Matt handed me the jacket. As soon as I touched it, I felt like I was traveling through a tunnel. Then I saw Amber in the bus window again, as clearly as if I were watching TV.

She still lay on the ground. Her hand was near her face, and she wore a charm bracelet. The red bruises on her arm were shaped like fingerprints. Someone had held her too tight. Past her, I saw the cliff beyond. The town lights twinkled below in the evening light.

I *did* know where Amber was. She was at the lookout on the top of Little Mountain.

Was she alive? I tried to focus on her face, what I could see of it under her hair. There was blood on her forehead. She appeared to be unconscious, knocked out. Yet she was still breathing. "Oh, thank god," I said.

"What?" asked Matt.

As soon as I heard him speak, I lost the vision. I saw only myself in that window now. I looked like I felt: scared. I feared for Amber's safety, but I also feared for my own. Why was this happening to me? The vision left me feeling dizzy and shaky.

Still, I had to focus on Amber. I had to save her. "I was right," I told Matt. "I know where Amber is. She's still alive, but hurt. I saw her lying on the ground near the Little Mountain viewpoint."

"Way up there?" Matt asked. "Amber couldn't have walked all that way on foot." He frowned. "How do you know where she is? Where is she now?"

"Still there, I expect."

Matt shook his head. "I don't understand. You saw her there, lying on the ground, and didn't think to drive her down? What is the matter with you?"

"I wasn't there, exactly," I said.

"Did you see her at the viewpoint or not?"

"I saw her there, but I wasn't there myself." At least, my body wasn't, I thought. I felt like some part of my mind had traveled to find Amber. "They call it *remote viewing*," I told him.

Matt shook his head. "I don't understand."

"When I held Amber's jacket earlier and again just now, I saw—" I paused. There was no way out of this. I had to tell him. "I had a vision of her."

Matt laughed. "A *vision*? You mean like the visions your mom has? Hell, she's forever phoning me up, telling me where to find some lost tourist. All because she saw the poor slob in one of her 'visions.' I won't take her calls anymore."

"I know it sounds goofy," I said. "But I swear that's where Amber is."

Matt rubbed a finger over the stubble on his upper lip as he thought for a moment. "I heard the cops, ambulance drivers and firefighters call you Radar," he said. "You turn up at accident scenes before they do."

"Sometimes," I said, trying to make less of it. Then I nodded, admitting the truth. "Often."

"I take it you have these 'visions' often too."

"No, I've never experienced anything like this before," I said. "I've only had hunches, gut feelings. I'll *know* I have to turn down a certain road. Then there'll be an accident on that road in front of me."

I glanced down at Amber's jacket in my lap. "This time was different. I *saw* Amber as clearly as I'm seeing you."

"You were imagining things." He paused. "Or hallucinating."

"I'm not seeing things, not in that way. I'm not crazy. I can prove it to you."

"I don't have time for this," Matt said. "There's a girl missing on that mountain." He took Amber's jacket from me. "We're into winter, and Amber doesn't even have this to protect her."

"Matt, please listen to me," I begged. "I *know* that's where she is."

"Go home, Claire," Matt said. He looked down at my bare legs under my short skirt. "And put on something warm so you don't freeze to death yourself." He went back to studying his map. "I don't want to have to rescue you too."

I raked a hand through my hair as I searched my memory of the vision. I had to convince Matt that what I saw was real. "She was wearing a charm bracelet," I told him. "One of the charms was a tiny boat."

Matt turned back to me, shocked. "Who else were you talking to?" he demanded. "How did you know she was wearing that bracelet?"

"No one," I said. "Jim told me Amber was missing. Then I came here and talked to you."

"Then how could you know about the boat on that bracelet?" He peered at me, angry. "Did you talk to Amber's mom before you got here?"

"No. Like I said, I saw it."

"In a vision."

"Yes."

Matt paused a moment, then took my elbow. "Come on."

He led me outside the bus. I trotted beside him in my high heels as he strode to his pickup truck. "Where are we going?" I asked him.

"Up to the Little Mountain viewpoint," he said.

"You believe me?"

"No."

"Then why—?"

"The truth is, we haven't had any luck tracking Amber," he told me. "The police dog hasn't picked up her scent. Temperatures are dropping. If we don't find her in the next couple of hours, she'll freeze to death. I'll take any lead at this point, no matter how silly it sounds."

"Aren't you taking a team of searchers with you?" I asked.

"I said I'd check out your story, but I'm not going to waste our volunteers' time. Amber was last seen jogging this wilderness trail. That's where we'll focus the search." He opened the passenger door of his truck for me. "I'll take you up to the viewpoint myself."

I hesitated before getting in his truck. "The last thing I want to do is waste your time," I said.

"You've already done that." Matt got into the truck and lifted his chin at me. "Get in," he said.

FOUR

As Matt drove up the logging road, he glanced at my high heels. "You're not exactly dressed for this," he said. When I saw him check out my cleavage, I buttoned my jacket over my white blouse.

Matt turned to face the road ahead of us, embarrassed. "But you look good," he added. He lowered his voice. "Really good."

"Thanks, I think," I said. *He* looked good too, though I wouldn't tell him that. He had a day-old beard, and it suited him. Then, of course, there was his search-and-rescue jacket. I admit, I'm a sucker for a guy in uniform.

I'm sure that's the real reason I agreed to go out with Trevor. There's nothing sexier than a man in firefighting gear. Trevor even had his photo in a pinup calendar the fire department sold to raise funds. Dating him made me feel important.

The thing is, Trevor and I had never got past that goodnight kiss. Then again, if I stopped standing him up, we might end up in bed.

Matt and I reached the top of Little Mountain. "Stop here," I told him, pointing at a turnout in the road. "This is the place." I could feel it. "I saw Amber by the cliff. I saw the lights of the town below."

Matt pulled over, and I stepped out onto the gravel road. The forest around us smelled of pine. Snow had begun to fall. We were supposed to get several inches that night, the first real snowfall of the season.

I led Matt down a narrow path through the woods to the edge of the cliff. This was the viewpoint, overlooking the town of Black Lake. Young lovers often parked here. Teens partied here. Every couple of years, some drunk kid stepped off this cliff to his death.

"This is the place," I told Matt. Below us, the lights of town glittered around Black Lake as sunset painted the clouds orange. The view was exactly what I'd seen in my vision, but Amber wasn't there.

"She was lying right here." I pointed at the ground where the pine needles were swept to the side.

"Someone—or something—has been here recently," Matt said. "Could have been a deer taking a nap. Could have been kids making out."

"Amber could have been here too, right?" I asked.

In answer, Matt cupped his hands to his mouth. "Amber," he cried. "Amber!"

We both listened, hoping for a reply. There wasn't one.

"She was unconscious," I said. "She couldn't answer our call."

"We don't know that," said Matt. "And she's not here, is she? If she was unconscious, how did she walk away?" His face was grim. Now he *really* didn't believe me.

"She *was* here," I told him. "Could she have fallen from the cliff?"

"There are no footprints or any sign that anyone has been over there."

I peered at the ground, hoping to find a footprint to show him. "Check this out," I said, following the path. The forest floor was swept from the viewpoint all the way back to the road. "Looks like something heavy was dragged out of here," I told Matt.

I shuddered at the thought. Did someone—or something—drag Amber away? "You don't think a bear got her, do you?" I asked.

"First you thought a kidnapper took Amber, now a bear." Matt shook his head. "You're really fishing for news, aren't you? Isn't the story of a lost girl enough?"

"It's not like that," I said. "I don't care about the news story. I just want to find Amber. I *know* she was here."

I hunted for clues, something to make Matt believe me. There was nothing. Only those drag marks through the pine needles. "She must have been moved," I said. "What if it wasn't a bear? What if a person dragged her away?"

"Your kidnapper?" Matt raised an eyebrow like he thought I was a fool.

"Yes!" I said. "There must be someone else involved." I scanned the road. There were fresh tire tracks in the mud. "There *was* another vehicle here recently."

"So a bunch of dumb kids came up here to party. They dragged their beer cooler back to their car. Mystery solved."

I was nearly in tears, I was so frustrated. "I know there is more going on here," I told him. "I *know* it."

Matt put a hand on my shoulder. "Amber went for a walk and got lost. This is a huge forest. Even experienced hikers get lost here. We rescue them every year."

"She's not simply lost."

Matt held out both hands. "How do you know?"

I shook my head. "I can't tell you. I don't know how I know. I just *know*."

Matt opened the door to his truck. "All right, that's enough," he said. "We're leaving."

He got in and slammed his door shut, leaving me outside. I searched one last time for a clue to offer him, but I didn't find anything. Finally, I got in the truck.

We drove back to the search-and-rescue camp in silence. Matt parked the truck by his command unit, the old bus. "I'm sorry," I said. "I was so sure Amber was up there."

Matt got out of the truck without saying a word.

"Can I hold the jacket one more time?" I called out to him. "Maybe I'll see more detail in my vision this time. Maybe I'll see where she was moved to."

Matt turned to me. "Go home, Claire." He shooed me away. "Or go have that date with Trevor."

"I want to help." I tottered after him in my silly heels. "You don't understand. I *need* to help."

"There's nothing you can do."

"Please," I said. I took his arm, gripping it harder than I meant to. "I have to be here. I'm *supposed* to be here."

Even as I said that, I knew how nutty I sounded. I had no idea where Amber was at that moment. I couldn't explain those visions. Still, the feeling I had was so powerful. I *knew* Amber would die that night if I didn't help find her.

34

Matt stared down at his arm until I removed my hand. "I want you out of my camp," he told me. "Now."

FIVE

After I left the search-and-rescue camp, I went straight to my mom's house. I had to tell her about the vision I'd just had. Maybe she could help me figure out what to do. "Claire!" Mom said as she opened the door. "What a nice surprise." Mom was sixty-something but still fit. Yoga was her thing. She made a living teaching classes in her living room. In her black T-shirt and yoga pants, she appeared a lot younger than she was.

She waved me into the kitchen. "Didn't you have a date tonight?" she asked.

"I never made it to the restaurant," I said.

I swung my camera bag onto the kitchen table. Mom ran her business from here. This table was her desk. I shifted her laptop computer over a little and sat.

"You stood Trevor up *again*?" Mom asked. "For heaven's sake, Claire. He's the only man who's asked you out in a year. I do want grandchildren, you know."

"I know, I know. Now I'm afraid to phone him."

"You didn't let Trevor know you weren't coming?"

"No. I meant to, and then all this shit happened." Mom eyed me primly. I was thirty-one, and she still gave me hell for swearing. "All this *stuff* happened," I corrected myself.

"It's a wonder he didn't call *you*," Mom said.

"Yeah," I said, growing angry. "Why didn't Trevor call me?" I searched my camera bag for my phone to see if he had. Maybe in the confusion of the evening, I had simply missed his call. Then I realized I had left my cell plugged in and charging at home.

"Interesting," Mom said.

"What's that supposed to mean?"

"You 'forget' to call Trevor. You leave your phone at home so he can't call you. You clearly don't want Trevor to reach you."

"I like Trevor," I said.

"I'm just saying maybe there's a reason you stand him up so often."

I pointed at the camera bag sitting on the table between us. "My job is the problem," I said. "If I see news, I have to get the story. I'm simply busy, that's all."

"Trevor is a volunteer firefighter, Claire. He runs his own car-repair shop. *He's* busy. Yet he always turns up for your dates."

I thought for a moment. Mom was probably right. I did keep avoiding my dates with Trevor. But why? Trevor was good-looking, kind and a *firefighter*.

"So why didn't you get to your date with Trevor this time?" Mom asked. "What was the big news story?"

I told Mom about the gut feeling that led me to that burning car. Then I explained how I ended up at the search-and-rescue camp. I told her about my visions of Amber and my trip up the mountain with Matt. "I know what I saw in those visions was real," I said. "I'm so sorry I didn't believe you when you told me about your visions."

She patted my hand. "That's okay, dear. No one else believed me either. You have to experience the visions yourself to understand."

"That's just the thing," I said. "Matt doesn't believe me. Who will?" I cradled my head in my hands. "I know Amber will die if I don't find her. The question is, what do I do now?"

"You haven't eaten anything this evening, have you?"

"No," I said.

"You can't think on an empty stomach. I'll make you something."

I mulled over the events of the evening as she threw together a cheese sandwich. "The vision scared me," I said.

"You feel like you're not in control of your own mind," Mom said.

"Yes!"

"I know. You will get used to it, over time."

"Why is this happening to me? Why now?"

Mom shrugged. "Who knows? Your grandmother had visions. So did your aunt May. All the women on my side of the family had the gift."

"It doesn't feel like a gift," I said. "I know it's selfish to think about it right now, but I'm afraid my reputation is ruined.

Matt thinks I'm crazy. The whole town will hear about my visions now. Everyone will think I'm a flake."

"Like me," Mom said.

"I didn't say that."

"You didn't have to." She handed me the sandwich. "In any case, I don't think you have to worry about your reputation. I knew Matt's father. He hated gossips. I suspect Matt is a lot like him. Matt has never told anyone about the visions I had."

"He told me. He said he wouldn't take your calls anymore."

"Well, he damn well should. I knew where that Evans boy ran off to last month. I knew where that awful man hid that little girl in 2011—well, at least before he moved her. I knew where that teenager drowned during the summer of 2012."

"Matt didn't find the body where you said it would be."

Mom crossed her arms. "I said I knew where she *drowned*, not where her body ended up, downriver."

I pushed the sandwich away. I didn't feel like eating now. "Matt didn't believe you any of those times. He still doesn't."

"People rarely do. You'll find you can't stop yourself from trying to help anyway. You'll feel driven to."

"Like I do right now," I said.

Mom patted my hand. "You need to go. You *must* find that girl."

"I can't go back to the search-and-rescue camp. Matt won't listen. I'll only embarrass myself even more."

"You can't let this go," Mom said. "A girl's life is at stake." She paused. "And you have a chance here to prove that neither of us is crazy."

She was right. My mother's honor was also on the line, not just my own. If my vision helped me find Amber, maybe

Matt and the rest of the town would take our visions seriously. But all of that didn't matter now. I just wanted to find Amber.

"I don't know what to do," I said. "Matt kicked me out of the camp."

"So don't go back there—at least, not right away."

I shook my head. "I don't follow."

"You said Amber's mom was at home. Stop in on her. Ask for a personal item that might trigger another vision. Choose something Amber wears a lot. That works best."

I laughed. This all sounded so unlikely. Here I was, talking with my mom about how to spark a vision. "Any more tips?" I asked, making a joke of it.

Mom wasn't in a joking mood. "You can't force yourself to have a vision," she told me. "You must be relaxed. Hold the personal item. Then breathe deeply and allow your mind to take you where you need to go."

"You're asking me to meditate on the object?"

"Well, yes."

"Helen will definitely think I'm crazy," I said.

"Of course she will," said Mom. "You'll just have to find a way to convince her you're not."

SIX

Amber's mom lived in the apartment above the bakery she owned. I rang the bell at the bottom of the stairs and waited. I rang again. Eventually, I heard slow footsteps coming down the stairs.

Helen opened the door, wearing jeans and a T-shirt. Her face was tense with worry. She looked me over as if she wasn't sure what to make of me. I was still wearing the red miniskirt and high heels.

"I'm sorry to wake you, Mrs. Miller," I said. "I've come about your daughter."

Her face lit up with hope. "They found Amber?"

"No, I'm afraid not."

Her shoulders fell. Then she grabbed my arm, panicked. "They didn't find her body, did they?"

I shook my head. "I'm not from Search and Rescue, Mrs. Miller."

"I'm Helen," she said. "Call me Helen."

I extended my hand. "I'm Claire Abbott. I work for the *Black Lake Times*. We talked when you first opened your bakery."

"Yes, of course. I remember you now."

"May I come in?" I asked.

She started to close the door. "I can't talk about Amber right now. I just can't."

"I'm not here to talk about Amber for a news story."

She shook her head in confusion. "I don't understand."

"I just want to help find her. May I see Amber's room? I need a personal item, something that belongs to her."

Helen's voice rose in alarm. "You want to snoop around in my daughter's things?"

"No, I—"

"What do you want?" she cried. "Why are you here?"

"I had a vision," I told her. "I knew where Amber was, at least at that moment. Matt and I went up to Little Mountain viewpoint to find her, but she was gone."

Now Helen grew angry. "Why are you doing this to me? Go away!" She slammed the door in my face.

"Mrs. Miller," I called. "I don't think Amber is simply lost. I think someone kidnapped her."

I heard her footsteps pause partway up the stairs.

"She was wearing a charm bracelet," I called through the door. "One of the charms was a little boat."

I heard her step back down the stairs. She opened the door. "How could you possibly know that?" She hesitated, then opened the door wide. "Come in," she said.

I followed her up the stairs and into the apartment, a loft. I could see the doors to the upstairs bedrooms from the open space below. The kitchen and living area were in one room with a very high ceiling. The place smelled of bread from the bakery below.

"You said you need a personal item," she said.

"Yes, to trigger a vision."

"You're some kind of psychic?" she asked.

"No. At least, I don't think so. I can't tell the future or anything. I just get these hunches. Earlier when I touched your daughter's jacket, I saw her. I knew she was at the Little Mountain viewpoint. But, like I said, when we got there she was gone."

"How do you know she was really there in the first place?"

"I just know," I said. "I saw her."

"In your vision." She raised an eyebrow.

"Look, I know how crazy this sounds," I said. "But please let me try. I know I can help find your daughter. I just need to hold something that belongs to Amber."

Helen nodded her head as she thought that over. Her face was pale with grief. "I'm desperate," she said. "I'll try anything." She ushered me to the stairs. "This way," she said.

I followed her up to Amber's bedroom, a typical teenager's room. The walls were painted pink and purple. The same colors were on the bedding. Amber had left her jewelry, makeup and clothes spread all over.

"What do you need?" Helen asked.

"I don't know," I said. "Anything." Then I remembered what Mom had told me. "Something she wears all the time."

"She wears this necklace every basketball game." Helen held up a small silver heart on a chain. "Her dad gave it to her before he died. She says it brings her luck."

"Perfect," I said. I took the chain from her and focused on Amber's dresser mirror. I felt that strange feeling again, as if I was rushing down a waterslide. And there, in that mirror, I saw Amber.

This time she lay on a floor in a small room. The floor was moving up and down and from side to side. I squinted, trying to make sense of what I saw. There was a seat beyond her.

"She's in a van," I said.

"What kind of van?" Helen asked.

As soon as she spoke, I lost the vision. "I'm not sure," I told her. "An older one." I shook my head. "There was something on the walls. Carpet. But that doesn't make sense."

"That makes perfect sense," said Helen. "Doug drives a van like that, with shag carpet on the inside walls."

"Doug Conner?" I asked. "Amber's old boyfriend?"

Helen nodded. "He fixed up his van like one of those 1970s custom vans. He even has a bed in the back. When they were still dating, I told Amber I didn't want her in that thing. You can understand why."

I sure did. The kid had a bedroom on wheels. "Amber did break up with Doug though, right?" I asked.

"Yes, a couple of weeks ago. Doug wasn't very happy about it. He turned up at the bakery, trying to talk to her. I had to tell him to leave."

"Did you tell Matt about that?" I asked.

"Well, no. It didn't seem important. Doug didn't come back after that. Amber said he was behaving himself at school. He left her alone."

"Do you have any reason to believe he would hurt her?"

"I don't know. Amber said he pushed her once during their breakup argument. He's a moody kid. I thought he was depressed. I worried he was taking something."

"Drugs?"

Helen nodded. "I talked to Amber about that. She thought he sometimes got into his Mom's pills. I urged her to stay away from him for that reason. Eventually, she listened."

Helen thought for a moment. "Amber just started seeing Liam Peterson this past Friday," she said. "I suppose that could have made Doug jealous. I know he was suspicious of Liam's interest in Amber in the past."

"Jealous enough to kidnap her?"

Helen put her hand over her mouth. "I don't know," she said.

She pointed at the necklace in my hands. "Do you know where they are now?" she asked.

"They were driving down a logging road, through trees. I think they're still in the Little Mountain wilderness area."

"Try again," said Helen. "Maybe you can see more."

I squeezed the necklace and willed a vision to come, but I saw nothing. I put the necklace down and tried a comb, a set of earrings, a bracelet. "I'm not getting anything," I said.

Then I remembered what Mom had said—I couldn't force myself to have a vision. I could only remote view when I was relaxed. Here I was, standing with a grieving mother and trying to prove I wasn't crazy. I was anything but relaxed.

"At least we know Amber is in Doug's van," Helen said.

"So you believe me?" I asked.

"Maybe," she said. "I don't know how else you could have known about Amber's bracelet, or the inside of that van." She picked up Amber's necklace and held it out for me to take with me. "Yes, I think I do believe you."

I sighed with relief. "Okay," I said. "Now all we've got to do is convince Matt."

SEVEN

Snow fell hard as Helen and I arrived at the search-and-rescue camp. We jumped out of my car and ran to the bonfire where Matt was talking to a group of searchers.

As I reached Matt, my heels slipped in the snow, and he grabbed me just before I fell. That was the second time I'd ended up in Matt's arms that evening. "I told you to stay out of my camp," he said.

I smiled weakly at the volunteers around us. I saw them whispering to each other and eyeing my short skirt and heels. They were all in full winter gear.

"Can I have a moment?" I asked Matt. "In private?"

He shook his head. "I want you out of here, now." Matt turned to Helen. "What has Claire been telling you?"

Helen put a hand on his arm. "Listen to what she has to say, Matt. She can help us."

"I know why you can't find Amber on the trails," I told him.

"And why is that?"

I looked again at the volunteers and stepped away, waving for Matt to join me. I didn't want the rest of the crowd to hear what I had to say. Helen followed us.

"All right," Matt said. "You got your privacy. Now, what is it?"

I hesitated. I was about to accuse a teen of a serious crime, without proof. "Amber is in Doug Conner's van," I said. "I think he's moving her from place to place so you won't find her."

"We're back to your kidnapper story, are we? I suppose you saw this in one of your visions?"

"I did."

"I believe her, Matt," said Helen.

Matt's voice softened as he talked to her. "Helen, you're tired. Your daughter is missing. That kind of stress will mess with your mind. We have no reason to believe Doug took Amber."

"Claire saw the inside of Doug's van in her vision," Helen told him. "She described the shag carpet on the walls."

Matt shook his head. "How long has Doug had that van?"

"About five months."

"Isn't it more likely Claire just saw him driving around town?"

"I've never seen Doug's van," I said.

"You may not remember—"

"We're wasting time arguing," I said. "I think Doug hurt her, Matt. I don't know how badly."

"Do you hear yourself?" Matt asked me. "You've just accused an innocent kid of assault and kidnapping." Matt turned to Helen. "You can't possibly believe this woman."

At that moment, I heard my mother's voice. "And why the hell not?" I turned to find my mother marching toward us. "If I were you, I'd be hunting for that van right now," she said to Matt.

"Oh, here we go," said Matt. He already thought Mom was loony. Her bright pink earmuffs and silver puffy jacket only added to that image. In her yellow snow boots, she looked like an overdressed duck.

"Mom, what are you doing here?" I said.

She waved a hand at Matt. "I'm here to make sure this fool listens to you."

"Your help is the last thing I need right now," I said.

Matt pointed a finger at me. "And I don't want your help either," he told me.

"But I do," said Helen. "Matt, please. You haven't found Amber. I'm willing to try anything at this point. Maybe Claire can lead us to my daughter. Maybe not. But isn't it at least worth a try?"

"Let me tell you something, Helen," Matt said. "Nearly every time someone goes missing, Claire's mom phones us, claiming she knows where that person is. She's got a 'feeling.'" He made quotation marks in the air with his fingers.

Mom poked him in the chest. "If you'd just listen once or twice, you would come to believe me," she said.

"I did listen to you at first," said Matt. "You always ended up wasting our volunteers' time. That's precious time we could have used to track down those missing people."

"I told you exactly where that Evans kid was hiding last month."

"In the old Sterling mansion, I know," said Matt. "Except we found him in the Johnsons' barn."

"He was in that mansion when I told you he was there. He hid in the root cellar when he heard everyone looking for him. Then he left."

"I questioned him later," said Matt. "He was never there."

"He was lying," said Mom. "He broke into the Sterling mansion. He figured he'd catch shit if he told you that."

I raised my eyebrows at my mom, surprised that she had sworn. "Catch hell," she corrected herself.

Helen took a step closer to me. "Claire knew about the new charm I just gave Amber," she said. "The little boat. How could she have known that? I just gave it to my daughter this week."

"I imagine Amber wore that bracelet to school," said Matt.

"Yes, I guess she did."

"Isn't it possible Claire saw it then? She's often up at the school taking pictures."

"I haven't been up to the school this week," I told him.

"So you claim."

"I suppose Claire could have seen the bracelet and forgotten," Helen said.

Ah hell, I thought. Now Helen doubted my story too.

"Matt, please," I begged. "At least have the volunteers and cops search for that van. I'm sure Amber and Doug are still in the wilderness area. I saw blood on Amber's head, and she was unconscious. She clearly needs medical care. We've got to find that van before it's too late!"

Helen covered her mouth and sobbed when she heard me say that. Matt wrapped an arm around her. "I want you two out of

61

here—now," he told Mom and me. "Don't make me call the cops."

He turned his back on us and led Helen to the coffee tent.

I was nearly in tears too. I thought I could help Matt find Amber, but he wouldn't let me. He clearly thought I was nuts.

Worse, I was starting to doubt myself. Maybe I *was* just seeing things. Maybe I was as loopy as my mother.

"I'm so sorry," Mom said. "I made matters worse, didn't I? I should have kept my nose out of this."

"You were only trying to help."

"We should call the cops ourselves," she said. "Make them hunt for Doug's van."

"And when they ask why, what do I tell them? That I had visions? If Matt doesn't believe me, the cops sure as hell won't."

Mom shook her head. "You're right. They've never believed me either."

We both stared into the bonfire for a time. The warmth and crackle of the fire relaxed me a little. I put my hands in my pocket to warm them and felt Amber's necklace there. Almost immediately, I had another vision.

I saw Amber lying in the back of the moving van. Beyond her, I could see the front windshield and the back of a man's head. He turned to his right, and I saw his face. Yes, it was definitely Doug Conner.

Beyond, I saw a rough logging road in the dusky light. They were still on that mountain. I was absolutely sure of it.

"I just don't know what else to suggest," said Mom, and my vision ended. "I don't know what to do."

"I do," I said. I dangled Amber's necklace in front of her. Then I nodded at the mountain above us. "We go up there and find Amber ourselves."

EIGHT

I got Mom to drive my Honda Civic up the logging road. That way, I could hold Amber's necklace and focus on my visions. It wasn't the smartest decision I'd ever made. Mom was a nervous driver, especially on winter roads.

She hunched over the steering wheel and peered out the windshield at the snowy road. The windshield wipers couldn't keep up with the falling snow. She drove at a snail's pace.

"We'll never find Amber if you keep driving this slow," I told her.

"Look at that drop-off!" Her voice rose in panic. In the twilight, I could see the bank went straight down. "I go any faster, and we'll be in that gulley."

"Okay, okay," I said. "Just keep driving."

Mom glanced over at Amber's necklace in my hands. "Do you sense her? Are we going in the right direction?"

"I think so," I said. "She's still lying in the back of that van. But my vision of her keeps dropping in and out."

"It's all these damn trees and rocks," Mom said. "They're blocking your reception."

I laughed. "My reception? You're joking, right?"

"No," she said. "My remote viewing works like a walkie-talkie. Even a concrete wall can make it impossible for me to make a connection with the person. Get too far away from Amber, and you won't be able to see her at all."

I shook my head. This was all too strange. Still, I was starting to have a new respect for my mother. She continued to try to help people even as everyone made fun of her.

We drove farther up the mountain. Snow fell heavier now. A couple of inches of snow covered the dirt road, making it slippery. At one point, the Honda skidded to the side. Mom shrieked and yanked the wheel, just barely avoiding the drop-off.

She slowed down even more after that. "I can't drive in this," she told me. "You've got to take over."

"Wait," I said. "We're getting close." I could feel it. The hairs on my arms stood on end. I *knew* that van was just up ahead. We drove another couple of miles. "Pull over here," I told her.

Mom peered out the windshield at the snowy forest around us. "The van is here? I don't see anything."

"I think Doug's parked it around that bend. If we stop here, we can sneak up on him. We'll walk."

"Then what?"

I shrugged. "I don't know. I've never caught a kidnapper before."

"If he hurt Amber—" Mom didn't finish, but I knew what she was thinking. If Doug had hurt Amber, he could hurt us just as easily.

Mom wore snow boots. I was still in my high heels. She helped me up the snowy road. Within minutes, the skin on my legs went numb from the cold.

"Are you sure this is where it is?" Mom whispered.

"I'm sure." As soon as I said that, I slipped in the snow. Suddenly, I wasn't so sure anymore. What the hell was I doing here? I'd dragged Mom up this dangerous road even though I had no real proof that my visions were real. Was I just seeing things, as Matt thought?

Then we rounded the bend, and there was the van! The back of the vehicle was open. Doug Conner sat on the rear bumper, holding his face in his hands. He wasn't dressed for this weather either. He wore only jeans, a T-shirt and jean jacket.

Behind Doug, Amber lay on the mattress on the floor of the van. I held my breath, willing her to breathe, but she didn't move. I thought she was dead.

"Doug," I cried. "What have you done?"

Doug jumped up and waved a shotgun in my direction. "Get back!" he shouted. "I'll shoot."

"Claire," Mom said. She took my arm, warning me to back off. "That kid is stoned out of his mind."

She was right. Doug's eyes were glassy, and he appeared not just angry, but terribly confused. He clearly wasn't thinking straight.

Still, I shook off Mom's warning and stepped forward, holding out both hands. "Doug, put down the gun. We're here to help."

He squinted at me and my little red skirt. "Who the hell are you?"

"My name is Claire. Claire Abbott. I work for the *Black Lake Times*. I'm a reporter."

He shook his head, trying to make sense of things. "What are you doing here?" Then he aimed the shotgun directly at me. "I don't want this shit in the fucking newspaper."

"I'm not here as a reporter," I said. "I'm here to help. I know Amber is injured."

"She's not hurt," he said. "Not bad anyway. She's just sleeping."

"Sleeping?" I asked.

"I gave her some sleeping pills. My mom uses them lots. She'll be okay."

"How many did you give her?"

"I don't know. A few."

"Doug, you need to think about this," I said. "How many pills?"

"I don't know, I said!" His hands were shaking. He was the one holding the gun, but he was scared. Scared and stoned. That made him very dangerous.

"Did you take any pills yourself?" I asked him.

"Not sleeping pills."

"But you took something?"

"Yeah, what does it matter?"

"You took something from your mom's medicine cabinet? Do you know what?"

He shook his head as if thinking about this was too much work. "Just go away!" he shouted.

"I can't do that, Doug," I said. "I need to check Amber, make sure she's okay. You can overdose on sleeping pills. She could die."

I inched closer, with both hands out. "Just let me check Amber, okay? If she's fine, I'll back off."

He thought about that and signaled me over with the gun. I rushed to Amber's side and felt her pulse. I was no nurse, but I knew a weak pulse when I felt one. Her breathing was labored. Amber was in rough shape. "We need to get her to a hospital," I told Mom. "Now."

"Nobody is going to take Amber away from me," said Doug. "I want those search-and-rescue people off my back. I keep having to move. They just about caught up with me at the viewpoint."

So he and Amber *had* been there.

"I can't get off the mountain," Doug said. "They've got that camp set up down there, blocking my way."

He was right. The logging road we were on was a dead end.

"They're worried about Amber," I said. "We're all worried."

"They'll arrest me now, won't they?" he asked. "I don't want to go to jail!"

"You can take off into the bush. Go someplace where they won't find you. Wait there until this blows over. Just leave Amber with us."

"I'm not going to lose her again."

"If she doesn't get help, you *will* lose her. She'll die."

He stood there a moment, holding the shotgun in both hands. He seemed to be working out some kind of plan. "You got first-aid training?" he asked me.

"Some," I said.

"You're coming with me. You're going to take care of Amber."

"He has a gun," Mom said behind me. "Cooperate with him, Claire."

"Okay," I told him. "I'll take care of her."

"Give me your cell phone," he said.

"I don't have it on me," I told him. "I left it at home."

"I don't believe you. Nobody goes any-where without a phone. A reporter sure as hell wouldn't."

"Her phone is in her camera bag," Mom said quickly. "It's in the car." She was trying to calm him, give him a story he'd believe.

Doug aimed the gun first at me, then at Mom as he walked to my Honda. He snatched Mom's purse and my camera bag and threw them into the gulley. Now Mom couldn't phone for help. She'd have to drive down the mountain to get it. By that time, Amber might be dead.

Doug patted my pockets with one hand. When he was sure I didn't have a phone on me, he waved me into the van. He slammed the back door shut behind me.

Then he pointed the shotgun at Mom. "You tell Search and Rescue to back off," he said. "You tell them I've got a gun."

He jumped in the driver's seat and laid the shotgun across his lap as he started the van. I cradled Amber's head in my lap as we roared up the logging road. It would take Mom forever to drive back down that slippery mountain road. Even when she delivered Doug's message to Matt, I wasn't sure Matt could reach us in time to help Amber. I had to save Amber on my own. While I was at it, I had to save myself.

NINE

I was kidnapped! Shit. Doug was wasted on drugs and driving up a narrow logging road. The weather was getting worse. Snow was piling up, making the road even more dangerous. Amber's breathing was growing shallower.

I had to do something and do it quick, but what? Doug had a shotgun.

Maybe I could talk some sense into this kid. I kneeled between the front seats of the van. Doug immediately put one hand on the shotgun in his lap. "Where are you taking us?" I asked him.

"I've got to find someplace to hide," he said. "Like you said, we'll wait it out. Once the search-and-rescue guys are gone, we'll get off this mountain. Amber and me will take off."

"Do you really think she's going to want to go with you after all this?"

He didn't answer.

"Doug, turn this van around," I told him. "I know you don't want Amber to die. Take us back to the search-and-rescue camp."

"You can't tell me what to do!" He whined like a much younger kid. "I'm the one with the gun." He patted the shotgun. "I'm in control here. Not you."

I slumped back on the mattress in the back of the van. Amber groaned and shifted slightly. I turned her on her side, in case she threw up. That way, she wouldn't choke on her own vomit. I couldn't think what else to do for her.

I lifted Amber's arm to take a close look at the bruises there. They were red now but would turn purple by morning. Doug had clearly grabbed her arm hard enough to leave these marks.

"You hurt Amber," I told Doug. I checked her scalp. "Her head is bleeding. Did you hit her?"

"No!" he cried. "I love her. I took her up to Little Mountain viewpoint to tell her that. I packed a picnic."

"You knew she would be on the wilderness trail."

He nodded like he was proud of himself. "I know everything about her. She jogs there the same time every day. I parked close to the path and waited for her."

"You kidnapped her," I said.

"No!" He took his hand off the gun and slapped the steering wheel. "I just wanted to talk." I saw his face in the rearview mirror. He was anguished. I thought he might cry again.

"When she saw me on the trail, she told me to get lost," he said. "She just walked away from me like I was nothing."

"So you forced her into your van." Just like he forced me, I thought. With a gun. "Were you already stoned then?" I asked. "Doug, think about it. Would you have done any of this if you hadn't taken those drugs?"

He didn't answer for a moment. He seemed lost in the memory of that afternoon. The van skidded on the wet snow. Doug turned the wheel hard to keep the van on the road.

"She fought me and hit her head on the door," he said. "Why did she have to fight me? I never wanted to hurt her."

"You're hurting her now," I said. "Can't you see that?" I smoothed Amber's hair away from her face. "You gave her too many sleeping pills. If she doesn't get medical help, she will die."

"I only wanted to make her stay with me so I could talk to her. After I took her to the viewpoint, she tried to get away again. I stopped her and told her I'd take her home. I said we'd eat the picnic I made first. I made her drink the juice."

I pointed at the thermos on the front seat. "You put the sleeping pills in that," I said.

"Yes. We ate the picnic and she fell asleep. I had to drag her to the van." I thought of those marks on the ground that I'd seen at the viewpoint. So I was right about them. Doug had dragged Amber backward, covering his own footprints.

"Do something," Doug said. "Make her better."

"I'm not a nurse or a doctor," I said. "Even if I was, we would still need to get Amber to a hospital. If you don't take us back to the search-and-rescue camp right now, Amber will die."

"No!" he cried. "Fix her up. Do something for her!" The van slid to the side. Doug over-steered in the other direction and nearly drove into the bank.

"You're high on drugs," I told him as he drove on. "You shouldn't be driving."

"I'm fine."

"Let me take over. I'll drive Amber to the hospital. I can drop you off somewhere. You can take off."

"Shut up. Just shut up. You don't know shit. I'll never leave Amber."

I shook my head. "I don't understand why you are doing this."

"I love her."

"You have a funny way of showing it," I said.

"I told her I loved her. I told her I'd do anything for her." He started crying again. "She said she didn't care. She's seeing that asshole now."

"Liam Peterson, you mean."

"We only broke up a couple of weeks ago, and she's already with him. She must have liked him before, when she was with me." His hands gripped the steering wheel harder. "If she'd only listen, I could make her come back to me," he said. "I could make her love me."

"You can't make someone love you," I told him. "Especially not like this."

I glanced down at the girl's pretty face. "I don't think you're in love with Amber. I think you're in love with the *idea* of Amber. She's a basketball player. She's popular. You want to be popular, like her."

Sitting there in that van, I realized I was talking about myself as much as Doug. I had no real feelings for Trevor. I just liked the idea of him. I liked the idea of dating a *firefighter*.

"She's *got* to love me," Doug said quietly.

I just wasn't getting through to this kid. He was too drugged up and emotional to think clearly. There was no way I was going to talk my way out of this situation. I had to act, and act now.

I leaned between the two front seats and pointed out the driver's-side window. "Look out!" I cried, to distract him. Doug turned his head, and I grabbed the shotgun from his lap. But he caught me and yanked the gun out of my hand. He fired the weapon by accident as he did so, blasting a hole in the windshield.

"Shit!" Doug yelled. He dropped the gun to the floor and put up both hands to protect his face. I turned the steering wheel hard to the right so we wouldn't drive off the road. The van careened into the bank.

I heard the crunch of metal as the front end slammed into rock. My body was hurled to the floor between the seats with the impact. Then everything went deadly quiet.

TEN

I touched the bump growing on my forehead. No blood. I took a moment to make sure I was all in one piece before turning my attention to Amber. I knew from the pain that I would have bruises all over my body in the morning. At least I didn't seem to have any broken bones.

In the crash, Amber had rolled to one side of the van. The mattress she was on had cushioned her. She didn't appear to have any more injuries. She was still breathing, though her pulse was even weaker than before.

That drug overdose was killing her. I had to get her off this mountain. Fast.

Doug was quiet in the driver's seat, apparently knocked out. Blood dripped from his right hand, hanging limp by his side. I hadn't meant to cause the accident. I'd just wanted to get the shotgun out of his hands. At least I had accomplished that, I thought. The gun now rested on the floor between the seats, along with his thermos.

All I had to do was find Doug's cell and phone Search and Rescue. I just hoped Amber would hang on long enough for help to arrive.

I moved into the passenger seat and slid a hand into Doug's jacket pockets, searching for his phone. When I didn't find it, I opened the glove box to peer inside. Then I heard the click of the gun. I turned to see Doug pointing the shotgun at me. I shifted slowly in my seat to face Doug, with my hands in the air. There was blood on his forehead.

He must have hit his head against the dash. He favored his shoulder as if it hurt. Blood oozed from the gash on his arm.

"I don't think we're going anywhere now," I said. I turned his attention to the crunched front end of the vehicle. The headlights lit up the bank, but the engine was dead. "You've got a cell, right?" I asked him. "Let me phone for help."

"Get out," Doug told me. "Now."

I backed my way out of the vehicle and stood in the snow. Doug went around the back of the van to check on Amber. I followed. "We can still save her," I told him. "Just give me your phone."

"I'm not going to jail."

"You don't have to. Like I said, you can make a run for it. I'll take care of Amber."

"No!" he cried.

"Or stay, if that's what you want," I said. "You need help too." I touched his bloody arm. He staggered a little from the pain.

"You're not phoning anybody," he said. He slurred his words. Clearly, the blow to his head had left him even more confused.

"Listen to me carefully," I told him. "If we stay here, we'll all die of exposure. We'll freeze to death. Amber will die first. She's already close to death now."

"No!" he whined. "She won't die."

"She will, Doug. Give me the damn phone."

"No!" Doug dug his cell from his back jeans pocket and hurled it over the edge of the road.

"Why the hell did you do that?" I said. He aimed the shotgun at me. "No cops. No Search and Rescue. No one is coming between me and Amber. Nobody."

"Then Amber may very well die," I said. We had no way to call for help now. My only hope was that Mom had convinced the cops her story was true. Even if she had, I wasn't sure emergency crews would reach us in time.

Doug stumbled around in a circle, holding the gun to his shoulder as if trying to find a target. His eyes watered. "There's no way out of this," he moaned. "There's no way out."

"There's always a way," I said. "Please, give me the gun."

At that moment, I heard a car approaching. The vehicle's lights blinded us both as it rounded the bend. Doug flinched and turned away.

My mom jumped out of the driver's side, leaving the lights on. I realized only then that the car was mine.

"Claire!" Mom cried. "Are you all right?"

"What the hell are you doing here?" I asked her. "You were going for help, remember?"

She pointed her thumb at Doug. "I had to follow you," Mom said. "You know I did."

Mom had raced up that logging road behind us. I loved her for it, but now I was sure no one would help us.

Doug turned the gun on my mother. "You," he told her. "Give me your car keys." When Mom didn't hand them over right away, he shouted, "Now!"

"Okay, okay!" Mom tossed him the keys.

"Reporter lady," he said. "Get Amber into that car."

"Only if I'm driving her to a hospital."

Doug pointed the gun back at Mom. "Do it."

"This isn't like you, Doug," I said. "The drugs are messing with your mind. I know you don't really want to hurt any of us."

Doug fired the gun at Mom's feet to prove he was serious. The gunshot echoed off the hills around us. "Do what he says, Claire," said Mom. Her voice was tense.

I held both hands out. "Okay!" I said. "All right. Just calm down."

I struggled to lift Amber from the van. I put a shoulder under her arm and hauled her to the car. Then I slid her into the backseat of my Honda, clicking her seat belt in place.

Doug waved both Mom and me away with his gun, swaying as if he was having trouble standing. Then he got in my car and started it up.

"Doug, please get Amber medical care," I begged.

"You can't leave us here," said Mom. She pointed at my flimsy skirt. "We'll freeze."

Doug didn't reply. He slammed the car door shut and sped off past the van.

Mom and I watched my car disappear around the next bend. Cushioned by snow, the forest was eerily quiet. We were alone on that logging road.

"No one knows we're here, do they?" I asked Mom.

Mom shook her head. She started to cry as the reality of situation sank in. "Oh my god," she said. "What do we do now?"

ELEVEN

I took Mom's hand and strode with her to
Doug's van. "Come on," I said. "I'll tell
you what we're going to do."

I held the passenger door open for her.
"I'm going to find a way to stop Doug
before he kills both himself and Amber."

"How are we going to do that?" Mom
asked. "We can't catch him on foot."

"For starters, let's see if we can get this
piece of shit back on the road."

For once, Mom didn't bother to correct
my swearing. I got in the van. The keys were
still in the ignition. I turned the key, and after

the third try, the engine roared back to life. Within moments, heat poured from the vents.

"Hold on," I told Mom. I put the van in reverse and floored it. We fishtailed back onto the snowy road.

"Oh, thank god!" Mom said. "Now we can go back to the search-and-rescue camp for help."

"Nope," I said. I turned the wheel and headed up the logging road, not to the camp.

"No? Claire, what are you thinking?"

"Amber is in really bad shape," I said. "Search-and-rescue crews may not get to her in time. Doug is so stoned, he'll drive right off this road. We've got to stop him right now. I'm following him."

"He has a gun. You can't deal with him by yourself."

I peered at the road in front of me and gripped the wheel. "I have to," I said. "There is no one else." I glanced at Mom. "I'm sorry I dragged you into all this."

"How are you going to stop him?" Mom asked.

"I don't know," I said. "I'll figure it out."

"You can't drive this fast in these conditions," she said. "You can hardly see."

She was right. That shotgun blast had riddled the windshield with cracks. Only one wiper worked now. To make matters worse, the snow was really coming down.

On one side of the road, there was a rock face and the forest above. On the other, there was a sheer drop-off. The road up this mountain was steep. If we started sliding, we'd slip right off that cliff.

I felt the tires of the van skid as I turned a corner. I slowed briefly and shifted down to gain control. Then I sped up again on a straight stretch.

Up ahead in the dusk I saw my own car bouncing from side to side. Doug was stoned and a less experienced driver than me. He was having trouble keeping my

Honda on this slippery road. I quickly caught up with him. As soon as I did, he pressed his foot to the gas and took off.

"That kid is going to kill himself and Amber too," Mom said. "Pull back so he'll slow down."

I backed off a little, but Doug didn't reduce his speed. He flew up the mountain ahead of us.

"I've got to get in front of him," I said. "Force him off the road."

Mom sat up, clutching the armrests in panic. "You can't be serious!"

I stepped on the gas again and caught up with Doug. The road was narrow. As I attempted to pass the car, my tires came within inches of the drop-off.

Mom grabbed my arm in terror. "You're going to kill us!"

I turned the wheel sharply as we rounded the next bend, to avoid flying off that mountain. Doug and I were side by side now. Through my mother's window, I saw his face glow in the ghostly light of the car's dashboard. Amber was slumped in the backseat with her seat belt still on. I hoped she was still alive.

"Watch out!" Mom cried. Up ahead the road narrowed to a single lane as it rounded the next corner. If I didn't back off, I would drive right off that cliff. Yet I knew I had to stop this kid.

"Hang on," I told Mom and floored it.

"Claire!" Mom screamed.

I roared past Doug. Then I slid in front of him just as we reached the narrow point. I slammed on the brakes. There was no room for Doug to pass. In the side mirror, I saw my car skid toward me as Doug lost control of it. "Oh, shit," I said.

The Honda turned a circle, nearly sliding off the road. Then it smashed into the back end of the van, pushing us forward. Mom shrieked as we skidded toward the drop-off.

I was sure we were going over the bank and into the ravine below.

But the back end of the van stopped inches from the edge. Mom and I sat in silence for a few moments. I felt my heart banging in my chest. My hands gripped the steering wheel so tightly they hurt. I released the wheel and turned off the engine.

"You okay?" I asked Mom.

"I think so," she said. Then she yelled at me. "Don't you ever do that again!"

I didn't make any promises. We were in a terrifying situation, but I realized I found it thrilling too. I felt like I was doing what I was meant to do. I now understood why cops and emergency workers like Trevor and Matt loved their jobs.

I opened the door of the van and got out.

"Careful," Mom said. "Doug still has that gun."

I approached my own car slowly, with both hands up. The engine of my Honda was still running and the lights were on, blinding me. I couldn't see Doug. Did he have his shotgun trained on me? Was he about to shoot me?

"Doug?" I called. "You okay?"

He didn't answer. I inched forward. "Don't shoot. I'm only coming to see if you and Amber are all right."

I squinted into the car, then slowly opened the driver's door. Doug's face was turned toward me. His body was limp. He was out cold, but he still had a pulse. I reached down to the floor at Doug's feet and picked up the shotgun.

Amber stirred in the backseat. Thank god, I thought. She was groggy and confused, but still alive. "I want to go home," she said.

"I know," I said gently. "We all do."

TWELVE

Matt phoned for an ambulance as soon as we got back to the camp with the kids. The ambulance arrived within minutes.

Mom and I watched from the bonfire as the attendants took care of both Amber and Doug. Doug would certainly face charges once he recovered. I almost felt sorry for him. I knew he would feel terrible about what he'd done once he was sober.

Matt and Helen joined us by the fire, and Helen gave me a hug. "I don't know how to thank you," she said. "You saved my daughter's life. You have a gift, a real gift."

"Stronger than mine, I think," Mom told me. "You don't give up." She put a hand on my shoulder. "You realize the responsibility you carry now. You'll always be on call to help people."

"Like an emergency worker," I said.

"Yes, like Matt here." She turned to Matt. "*Now* do you believe my daughter?" she asked him.

"Mom," I said, warning her to keep quiet.

"Your mom is right," Matt told me. "I should have listened to you, Claire. We could have found Amber much earlier." He scratched his cheek, looking sheepish. "In fact, I'm thinking of calling on you in the future."

I was surprised. "You mean you want to use my visions to track people down?"

"You found Amber when we couldn't," he said.

Mom tapped her own chest. "Maybe you'll also listen to this crackpot next time she calls," she said.

Matt grinned. "Maybe," he said.

Doug was still unconscious, but Amber roused a little as Helen got into the ambulance with her. "Mom?" she said.

"I'm here, honey," said Helen. "Everything's all right now."

The attendants closed the doors of the ambulance and got in. I shivered as I watched the ambulance drive down the road. The snow had let up a little, but the evening was still cold.

"You must be freezing," Matt told me.

I tugged down the hem of my tiny skirt, ashamed of all the skin I showed. "You must think I'm ridiculous," I told him.

Matt took off his search-and-rescue jacket and draped it over my shoulders. "No, not at all," he said. "You really do look great tonight." He cleared his throat. "You're an amazing woman," he said. "Trevor is lucky to have you."

I grunted. Trevor hasn't had me yet, I thought. He probably never would now.

Matt gauged the expression on my face. "Things not so good between you and Trevor?" he asked. He sounded kind of hopeful, as if he liked that idea.

"I don't think Trevor is going to want to see me after tonight," I said.

Mom leaned in to Matt to explain. "This is the third time in two weeks Claire stood him up," she said.

"Huh," said Matt. He seemed to think that over. "You never got your dinner, did you?" he asked me.

"No, and I'm starving."

Mom looked from me to Matt and back again. Then she patted my shoulder. "I'll just leave you two alone," she said. She waved goodnight as she went to her car. Matt rolled back and forth on his heels until she was gone. He seemed a little nervous, I thought.

"I sure could use a burger about now. I bet you could too. I think I owe you that much. Interested?"

My heart raced, and I felt a thrill run through me. Matt had just asked me out on a date! Finally, I thought. I grinned up at him. "I thought you'd never ask," I said.

By the age of eighteen, **GAIL ANDERSON-DARGATZ** knew she wanted to write about women in rural settings. Today, Gail is a bestselling author. *A Recipe for Bees* and *The Cure for Death by Lightning* were finalists for the Scotiabank Giller prize. She also teaches other authors how to write fiction. Gail lives in the Shuswap region of British Columbia, the landscape found in so much of her writing. For more information, visit www.gailanderson-dargatz.ca.

DISCOVER GAIL BOWEN'S
CHARLIE D MYSTERIES

Charlie D is the host of a successful late-night radio call-in show, *The World According to Charlie D.* Each of these novels features a mystery that is played out in a race against time as Charlie D fights to save the innocent and redeem himself.